LITTLE BEAR'S FRIEND

LITTLE BEAR'S FRIEND

An I CAN READ Book®

by ELSE HOLMELUND MINARIK

pictures by MAURICE SENDAK

by the author and artist of LITTLE BEAR

HarperCollinsPublishers

HarperCollins®, 📖®, and I Can Read Book®
are trademarks of HarperCollins Publishers Inc.

Library of Congress Catalog Card Number: 60-6370
ISBN 0-06-024255-8
ISBN 0-06-024256-6 (lib. bdg.)
ISBN 0-06-444051-6 (pbk.)

09 10 11 12 13 SCP 20 19 18 17 16 15

To

Mother and Father

CONTENTS

LITTLE BEAR AND EMILY

Little Bear sat in the top
of a high tree.
He looked all about him
at the wide, wide world.

He saw the green hills.

He saw the river.

And far, far away

he saw the blue sea.

He saw the tops of trees.

He saw his own house.

He saw Mother Bear.

He could hear the wind sing.

And he could feel the wind

on his fur, on his eyes,

on his little black nose.

He shut his eyes,

and let the wind brush him.

He opened his eyes,

and saw two little squirrels.

"Play with us," they said.

"No time," said Little Bear.

"I have to go home for lunch."

13

He began to climb down,

and saw four little birds.

"Look at us," they said,

"we can fly."

"I can, too," said Little Bear,

"but I always fly down.

I can't fly up

or sideways."

15

He climbed down some more,

and saw a little green worm.

"Hello," said the little green worm.

"Talk to me."

"Some other time," said Little Bear.

"I have to go home for lunch."

He climbed all the way down,
and there he saw a little girl.

"I think I am lost,"

said the little girl.

"Could you see the river

from the treetop?"

18

"Oh, yes," said Little Bear,

"I could see the river.

Do you live there?"

19

"Yes," said the little girl.

"My name is Emily.

And this is my doll Lucy."

"I am Little Bear, and
I can take you to the river.
What is in that basket?"

"Cookies," said Emily. "Have some."

"Thank you. I love cookies."

"So do I," said Emily.

They walked along eating cookies
and talking,
and soon they came to the river.

"I see our tent," said Emily,
"and my mother and father."

"And I hear my mother calling,"
said Little Bear.

"I have to go home for lunch.
Good-by, Emily."

"Good-by, Little Bear.

Come back and play with me."

"I will," said Little Bear.

Little Bear went skipping home.

He hugged Mother Bear and said,

"Do you know what I just did?"

"What did you just do, Little Bear?"

"I climbed to a treetop,

and I saw the wide world.

I climbed down again, and I saw

two squirrels, four little birds

and a little green worm.

Then I climbed all the way down,

and what do you think I saw?"

"What did you see?"

"I saw a little girl named Emily.

She was lost, so I helped her

to get home.

And now I have a new friend.

Who do you think it is?"

"The little green worm,"
said Mother Bear.

Little Bear laughed.

"No," he said, "it is Emily.
Emily and I are friends."

DUCK, BABY SITTER

Owl was having a party.

Little Bear, Emily and Lucy

were on the way to Owl's house.

They came to the pond
where Duck lived.
And there was Duck,
baby sitting.

Little Bear looked at
all the ducklings.

He asked,

"Will the mother duck

be back soon?"

"Oh, yes," said Duck.

"Wait for me.

I can go to the party

as soon as she comes back."

Emily put Lucy down, and said,

"Oh, what darling ducklings.

I wish I could hold one."

"Just call them," said Little Bear.

"My goodness!" said Duck.

"I think I have lost one!"

Little Bear and Emily

began to look for it.

Little Bear looked at
the tall reeds.
He said,
"If I were a duckling,
that is where I would swim.
It would be like swimming
in a forest."

He looked in the tall reeds.

And there was the duckling,
swimming about,
having fun.

"Hello, Little Peep,

I see you,"

said Little Bear.

"Peep!" said the duckling,

and swam out to the others.

Just in time, too,

because his mother had come back.

"Hooray!" said Duck.

"Now I am free.

Now we can go to the party."

They went skipping along.

Emily said,

"I think ducklings are lovely."

"Yes," said Little Bear,

"and owlets are nice, too.

Owl says they are."

Emily laughed.

"Oh," she said,

"I love all little animals."

"Me too," said Little Bear.

THE PARTY AT OWL'S HOUSE

Little Bear, Emily, Lucy,

Cat, Duck and Hen

all came to Owl's party.

Cat looked at Lucy.

"Who is that?" he said.

"That is Lucy," said Little Bear.

"Lucy is Emily's doll."

"Yes," said Emily.

"And she tells me things.

She wants to tell me something now."

"What?" said Cat.

"I can't hear her."

Emily put her head down

to Lucy's head.

"What is she saying?" asked Hen.

37

"Yes, tell us," said Duck.

"She is saying," said Emily,
"that she wants to sit up here."
And Emily made Lucy sit
in a little tree.

"See?" said Little Bear.
"Emily knows what Lucy wants."

"Let's eat," said Cat.

Owl came out of his house.

He said,

"Here are the party hats.

Put them on."

So they all put on party hats

and laughed at each other.

Then they sat down to eat.

"Look at Lucy!" said Duck.

"She wants to come down!"

They all looked, and there was Lucy,

coming down all by herself.

"Oh—Oh!" cried Emily.

"Lucy will break."

And Lucy did break.

She broke her arm.

"Oh, Lucy!"

Emily was crying.

She picked up her doll,

and hugged her.

"Don't cry, Emily," said Little Bear,

"we can fix her."

"I'll get some tape," said Owl.

So Little Bear fixed Lucy.

"There," he said.

"Ask her how she feels now."

Emily put her head down to Lucy.

44

"She says she feels fine,"
said Emily.
"And she says you are
a very good doctor, Little Bear."

"Tell her thank you,"
said Little Bear.
"Any time she breaks an arm,
or a leg, I will fix it."

Owl laughed.

"No more today, please,"
he said.

Emily made Lucy sit down.

Hen asked,

"Is she saying something?"

"Yes," said Emily,

"she wants us to begin the party."
And that is just what they did.
It was a very fine party, indeed,
even for Lucy.

She said so herself.

47

"YOUR FRIEND, LITTLE BEAR"

Summer was over,

and Emily was saying good-by.

It was time to go

back to school.

Mother Bear baked a cake.

Little Bear made lemonade.

Mother Bear said,

"Let us eat up all the cake.

If we do, then it will not

rain tomorrow."

"Let it rain," said Little Bear.

"Emily will not be here tomorrow

to play with me."

"Anyhow," said Emily,

"we can eat up the cake.

And we can drink the lemonade."

49

So they ate the cake,

and drank the lemonade,

and talked and talked.

Then it was time

for Emily to go home.

Father Bear said,

"Don't let Lucy break

any more arms."

"Oh, no," said Emily.

Emily hugged her doll, and said,

"Lucy wants to say good-by, too.

Say good-by to Little Bear, Lucy."

Emily made Little Bear hold Lucy.

Then she said to him,

"Little Bear, you can have Lucy
for keeps.

I will give her to you."

"Oh—" began Little Bear.

But before he could say anything,

Emily took Lucy back again.

"Oops!" she said. "I forgot.

Lucy has to come to school with me."

Emily opened her pocketbook.

She took out a fine new pen.

"This is for you," she said.

"I want you to have it."

Little Bear took the pen.

"Thank you, Emily," he said.

56

He ran into his room,

and came back with a pretty toy boat.

"This is for you," he said.

"For keeps.

You can sail it in your bathtub."

"Thank you," said Emily. "I will.

Good-by, Little Bear.

See you next summer."

Little Bear stood at the door

till Emily was out of sight.

Two big tears ran down his face.

Mother Bear saw them,
and took him on her lap.

"My goodness, Little Bear," she said.
"You will be going to school, too,
and you will learn to write.
Then you can write to Emily."

"Little Bear can begin right now,"
said Father Bear.

He got out some paper, and said,
"Little Bear can write his own name."

"Yes," said Mother Bear,
"with his fine new pen."

She took Little Bear's paw in hers,
and helped him to begin—

That made Little Bear very happy.

He said,
"When can I write to Emily?"

"Soon," said Mother Bear.

And soon he did write to Emily,
like this:

Dear Emily:

It is snowing.

I love the snow.

I wish I could send you some.

Owl, Duck, Hen and Cat

send their love.

So do the ducklings.

I cannot wait for summer.

Your friend,

Little Bear.